Of Life: The Rollercoaster

Written by Emmy Woosley and Jody Hulsey
Illustrated by Sarah Truman

Print ISBN: 979-8-35090-366-9

Dedicated to our friend, who inspires us with her creativity, courage, and optimism.

For the strong and brave children who keep moving forward on the rollercoaster of life.

Hi!
My name is Evelli.

And just like you,
my life is not perfect.

It's full of purple, pink, and blue.

Up, Up, Up.
Another beautiful day.

Clear sky, purple track.
Everything is OK.

Things could not be better.

"Life is amazing!" I say.

Pink track straight ahead.
Happiness, hugs, and lots of hooray!

The colors around me are changing.
Where are we going today?

Slowing down, I feel different.
My smile is fading away.

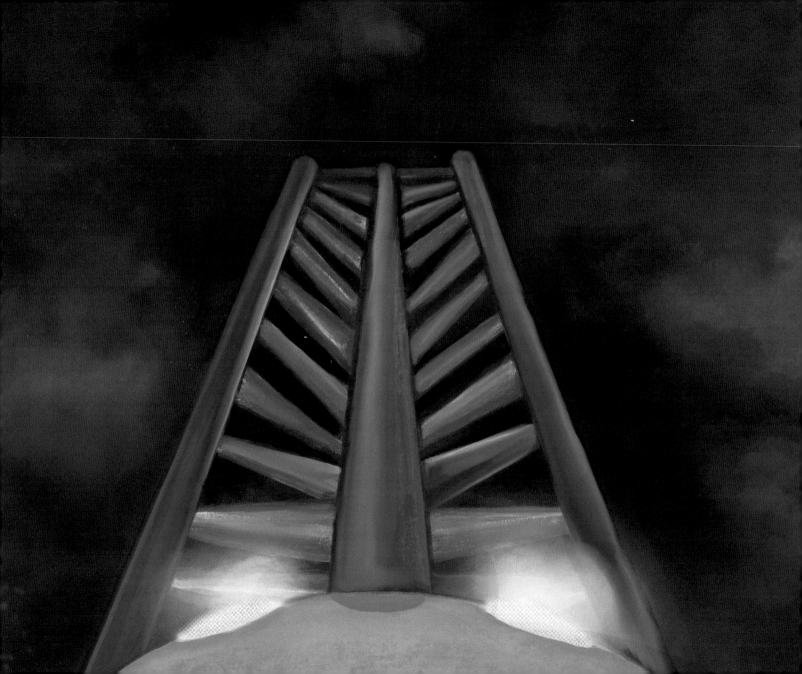

Fast, Fast, Fast.
Down the hill I go.

Is it safe?
I feel scared.

I must let someone know.

Twists and turns surround me.
I need a helper or a friend.

Dark tunnels, blue track.
Will this ever end?

Help is never far,
in my heart wherever I go.

I am Strong.
I am Smart.
I am Bold.

And they will know!

I may not have the power
to control my whole world,
but I can be optimistic
even for such a young girl.

Just then I see the clear sky.
Pink track is up ahead.

Climb, Climb, to the top.
"Life is amazing!" I said.

See, everything is beautiful.
Purple, pink, and even the blue.

That is what makes me special.
A gift to the world, just like you.

17

So Up, Up, Up we go.
Another beautiful day.

Clear sky, purple track.
Everything is OK.

Adapted from the poem "Of Life: The Rollercoaster" by Jody Hulsey

Up, Up, Up
Another beautiful day
Clear sky, purple track
Everything is OK

Things could not be better
"Life is amazing!" I say
Slowing down, I feel different
Where are we going today?

Fast, Fast, Fast
Down the hill I go
Is it safe? I feel scared
I must let someone know

Twists and turns surround me
I need a helper or a friend
Dark tunnels, blue track
Will this ever end?

Help is never far
In my heart, wherever I go
I am Strong, I am Smart
I am Bold and they will know

Just then I see the clear sky
Pink track is up ahead
Climb, Climb, to the top
"Life is amazing!" I said

See, everything is beautiful
Purple, pink, and even the blue
That is what makes me special
A gift to the world, just like you

So up, up, up we go
Another beautiful day
Clear sky, purple track
Everything is OK